COUNTING
SCARS

COUNTING SCARS

Melinda Di Lorenzo

orca soundings

ORCA BOOK PUBLISHERS

Published in Canada and the United States in 2022 by Orca Book Publishers.
orcabook.com

Library and Archives Canada Cataloguing in Publication
Title: Counting scars / Melinda Di Lorenzo.
Names: Di Lorenzo, Melinda, 1977- author.
Series: Orca soundings.
Description: Series statement: Orca soundings
Identifiers: Canadiana (print) 20210352981 | Canadiana (ebook) 2021035299X |
ISBN 9781459833555 (softcover) | ISBN 9781459833562 (PDF) |
ISBN 9781459833579 (EPUB)
Classification: LCC PS8607.I23 C68 2022 | DDC jC813/.6—dc23

Library of Congress Control Number: 2021949086

Summary: In this high-interest accessible novel for teen readers,
sixteen-year-old Adele finds herself in a complicated love triangle.

Orca Book Publishers is committed to reducing the consumption
of nonrenewable resources in the production of our books. We make
every effort to use materials that support a sustainable future.

Orca Book Publishers gratefully acknowledges the support for its
publishing programs provided by the following agencies: the Government
of Canada, the Canada Council for the Arts and the Province of British
Columbia through the BC Arts Council and the Book Publishing Tax Credit.

Design by Ella Collier
Edited by Tanya Trafford
Cover photography by Stocksy.com/Lucas Ottone and Getty Images/CSA Images

Printed and bound in Canada.

25 24 23 22 • 1 2 3 4

With many thanks to Brooke Carter,

for introducing me to the Orca pod

Chapter One

Ugly as shit.

That's my first thought when I see the welcome sign. It's big and brown with red lettering. The wood is worn, and the paint looks like it's been redone a hundred times. I hate it before I even read the words. And it gets worse when I do.

Welcome to Camp Happy!

The sickly-sweet name makes me want to cringe and roll my eyes. I keep the urge to myself. Not out of politeness. It's just self-preservation. I don't want to annoy the social worker in the driver's seat. I know for a fact she wouldn't appreciate a negative reaction. She's not a fan of rolling eyes. She also doesn't like raised eyebrows. Or sarcasm. Or black eyeliner. Or maybe she hates her job. Hell. There's even a possibility she doesn't like *me*. It's hard to say. She hasn't been mean to me, or even rude. She's just…bossy. Her pink lips are always tight. Even when she told me her name—which is Jane Cowley—she said it like it bothered her.

Do I care about any of that? Not really. Jane Cowley is the same as most grown-ups who are in charge of kids like me. They want to fix us. And we can't be fixed. We don't want to be. Deep down I think they know it, and this makes them tense. But it doesn't matter. Like I said, I don't care. Jane is just a person I have to put up with until this is over.

And I only have to do that for a few more minutes. Or that's what I'm counting on anyway.

Right now she thinks I'm asleep. My eyes are almost closed. My head is pressed to the window, and my breathing is slow. Everything I see is from under my eyelashes. I've been sitting this way for the last half hour. It's kind of uncomfortable, especially on my left wrist. I twisted it two days ago, and it still aches. I want to move it, but I don't dare. Pretending to be asleep helps me avoid conversation. Talking is the one thing Jane does like. And we don't have that in common. I'm happy to keep looking out the window in silence.

The trees pass in a green blur for a bit longer. But not long after I see the sign, I also catch my first glimpse of Camp goddamn Happy. A log cabin with a red roof peeks out from the forest. I notice right away that it matches the welcome sign, and I want to roll my eyes even more.

"Yes," I think again, "definitely ugly as shit."

I don't realize I've said it out loud until Jane jerks a look my way. Her whole body moves, and the seat bounces. Automatically I return her glance. *Damn.* Now she knows I'm awake. I don't turn away fast enough to hide it. Her blue eyes are laser sharp for that second.

"What did you say?" she asks, and her voice is the same as her expression.

Swearing is also on Jane's list of dislikes. High up there.

I do my best to smile.

"Nothing," I say. "Just that it's kind of ugly, isn't it?"

"I think they try for function. Not beauty," she replies.

I nod. Then I move my attention back to the window. I don't need Jane to read my face. She already knows too much about me. Like the fact my mom is in rehab. And about the month I've spent doing community service. Worst of all, she knows my dad was too busy to come and get me when everything went down. When I think about *that*—about my dad—my heart squeezes inside my ribs.

Why didn't he come?

"It's going to be fine, Adele," Jane says. "Trust me."

The idea of trusting her makes me want to laugh. Mostly because the idea of trusting *anyone* makes me want to laugh. A giggle tries to come out. I fight it back.

"Thank you," I reply in a serious voice.

Jane's fingers tap the steering wheel. Her mouth pinches in that way it does. If I had to guess, I'd say she's trying to decide if I mean it. She stays quiet, and I use the silence to study the rest of the camp. Most of it's visible now that the trees have cleared. I can see it well because we've come to the top of a hill.

Three log cabins are on one side of a wide path, and three more line the other side. At the far end of the path is a much bigger building, and to the left of it are two smaller ones. All of them are the same gross brown with red roofs. I finally let myself roll my eyes. It's a bit of a cover-up, though. I kind of hope it will draw attention from Jane. If she gets mad at me, it might distract me from the new nerves jumping around in my chest. But she doesn't get mad. She doesn't even get annoyed.

"I know you don't want to do this," she says.

"Oh, really?" I reply before I can stop myself. "What was your first clue?"

"Adele…"

"Jane."

"There was no alternative," she reminds me. "You have no family here. The terms of your probation include vetted supervision."

I tune her out. There's nothing she can say that I don't know already.

My mom's drug charge removed her from being able to supervise me. Possibly forever.

My friends' parents don't want a kid with a record living under their roofs.

I haven't seen my dad in ten years, and he wasn't excited to hear that I'm suddenly more than an expense.

Camp Happy is a last resort. It's a place run by the juvie courts. A final stop before people like Jane give up on people like me. No argument will make it any different. Not in a good way. The opposite is a possibility, though. They warned me about it when I was getting my wrist looked at in the hospital. I could be in a group home with a hundred other kids. I might have to go there if my dad doesn't get his shit together. But I don't let myself think about that last part.

Jane says I'm lucky. The judge who sent me here agrees. But I know better. These ugly brown-and-red buildings are a kind of prison. They just don't look like it from the outside.

Chapter Two

The car engine cuts out, and Jane says, "Wait here a second, sweetie."

I'm too surprised to answer her. In the last day and a half, she hasn't called me anything but Adele. Or maybe Ms. Reimer, the first few times. But right after she says "sweetie," she climbs out and slams the car door.

When she walks away, I stare at her. I narrow my eyes. Maybe surprising me was her plan. It sure kept me from asking any questions. I kind of want to jump out and follow her. But I don't. She might be expecting me to chase her. I'd rather not let her be right.

I don't stop watching her until she enters one of the small buildings. When I'm sure she's not coming back, I take a look around. Of course, the cabins haven't changed in the last two minutes. They're still brown. They still have gross roofs. And it's still the place I have to live for the next two weeks.

I don't want to think about that too much. It makes my heart want to do the squeeze thing again. It makes my throat hurt too. Quickly I search for something else to look at. And I find it. Actually, I find *him*.

A boy.

He's very tall. Neither fat nor skinny. He's looking down at a book. And for a minute, I think he isn't real. Why would a boy like that be standing there? He's too close not to have seen us arrive. I stare at him. If he's real, why doesn't he look up? It's weird.

I don't ask myself why I might see a fake boy reading a fake book. I just keep staring.

His tanned hands stick out from a long-sleeved gray shirt. His fingers flip a page. For some reason, I notice that he has wide knuckles. They make the book look small. I don't know why, but I like that. And liking it makes me blush.

I pull my eyes up from his hands. I want to see his face, even if it's not real. I see his hair instead. It's dark brown, almost black, except for a red stripe in the front. That piece hangs down over his forehead. My eyes stay there for a long time. I want the wind to blow the hair out of my way. It doesn't happen. I give up and move on with my stare.

He's got torn jeans. Dark, dark blue. They're tucked into unlaced combat boots. One purple sock sticks up on his left ankle. A red bandanna hangs from his pocket.

His fingers move again. This time one catches on the page. He sucks in a breath. He jerks his hand away and lifts it up. I see the same thing he does. A fresh line of blood. That's when I decide he's real. A paper cut isn't something I would make up.

His head tilts. I need to look away. If I don't, the very real boy is going to see me staring. But my eyes have their own ideas. They stay where they are, stuck on him. And he does look. Of course. He gazes right at me, and I blush harder. My cheeks are hot. But I still don't stop watching him.

His eyes are a dark color. I'm not sure what shade. Maybe they're brown, maybe green, maybe hazel. They hold me. My skin prickles in a strange way. My stomach does a roll. It's not a bad feeling.

It's like when I'm going down in a roller coaster. Scary and fun at the same time. The feeling stays even when the boy spins on his heel and walks away.

I have to go after him.

It's like I have no choice.

I swing open the door. But I forget to undo my seat belt. I'm stuck.

"Shit," I say.

My hand goes to the button. It takes two tries to get it open. By the time I'm free, the boy is gone.

Where did he go?

I fling a look back and forth. He didn't pass the car. He didn't head toward the end of the path. He must have slipped behind the cabin.

I take off, almost running. I get to the other side of the cabin but I don't see him. I stop. I look around again. Seriously. Where is he? I start to move, but a voice stops me.

"You don't want to follow that guy," it says.

I spin around. There's another boy standing beside the cabin. He's nothing like the first boy. This one is shorter, only as tall as me. He's blond. As good-looking as an underwear model. His shorts are khaki, his shirt the button-up kind with a collar. An oversize watch is on one wrist, glinting in the sun. And he's smiling at me. But my skin prickle is gone now.

"That's Fergus," he says. "And he's bad news."

"Bad news?" I reply.

It sounds weird, coming from someone my age. Our age.

"I mean, everyone here is bad news," the boy tells me. "But Fergus is kinda extra bad."

I don't know what else to say, so I say, "Oh."

"Are you new?" he asks.

"Yes," I reply. "I guess I am, I mean. Are there people here who aren't new?"

"Some of us are here for four weeks," he says. "What's your name?"

"Adele."

"I'm Andy."

He puts out his hand. I stare at it without moving.

"You're supposed to shake it," says Andy.

I lift my fingers and let him take them. His skin is warm. His grip is strong. He shakes. Up. Down. Like it's normal. Hell. Maybe it *is* normal. I've just never had a real reason to shake hands.

"Want some camp survival tips?" he asks.

"Sure," I say.

"First. Girls aren't allowed on this side."

"What?"

Andy points to the cabin beside us.

"These are for the guys," he says. "The ones on the other side of the path are for the girls."

"What happens if I'm on the wrong side?" I ask.

"I don't know," he tells me. "I don't break the rules."

He smiles again. His teeth are even and white. Perfect. It makes me wonder what he did to get sent here.

His face goes serious.

"Second tip?" he says. "It's what I said before. Stay away from Fergus. I've known him for a long time. If you follow him, you'll get hurt."

I want to ask him what he means. I don't get to. Jane is calling me. I turn toward her voice. Then I turn back to say goodbye to Andy. But now he's gone too.

My stomach churns again, but this time it's different.

Something bad is going to happen before I leave Camp Happy. I can feel it.

Chapter Three

I stay where I am for another second. I try to shake the sick feeling in my stomach. It doesn't want to leave.

Jane calls me again, and now she's yelling. I tell myself to forget those boys and run back to the car.

From there things move quickly. The bad feeling goes away, probably because I don't have time to think about it.

Jane gets my bag from the trunk. She takes it to one of the small buildings. There she introduces me to the four camp counselors, who go over the rules. No smoking. No drinking, no drugs. No hanging out with the boys unless it's a camp activity. A bunch of other obvious stuff. But I swear Jane smiles at each thing on the list.

I nod at everything. But my mind wanders. It goes to Fergus. What was he reading, and where did he go? Is he inside one of the boys' cabins? What did Andy mean when he said he was bad news? And why do I even care? I'm only here for two weeks. I don't need to make friends. I *really* don't need to get into any kind of trouble. Not in the form of a boy or anything else.

Get in. Get out.

I squeeze the hand on my uninjured wrist. I tell myself this will work. I can put the past away. And my dad can too.

The counselors keep talking. They move on

from the rules, and they tell me how many kids are at the camp. *Twenty-four.* Twelve girls, twelve boys. They tell me I'm lucky. Just like the judge and Jane did. Another girl was supposed to have this spot, but she canceled. I want to ask if she dropped out or got kicked out. But I don't do it.

When they finish—and it takes forever—they make me sign a contract. I try not to think I'm signing my life away too.

And suddenly Jane is ready to go. The camp counselors and I follow her to her car. She tells me goodbye, and that's it. She drives away without looking back. I watch her go. My throat scratches in the way it does before I cry.

Why do I feel sad?

It doesn't make sense. This is what I want. What I've been waiting for. I didn't like the way her eyes were always on me, always judging.

Maybe I'm sad because Jane's a known factor. She's been at my side for almost every minute for the last thirty-six hours. She was with me when the police came to my mom's house. And at the hospital, I saw her more than I saw the nurses and doctors. She might not like me, but she knew everything. Now...I have to start over.

The car is gone, and one of the camp counselors, Anna, puts a hand on my shoulder. She's a short woman with her hair cut into a blond bob.

"Are you ready to meet your bunkmates?" she asks.

Her voice is as cheerful as her face. Does she mean it? For some reason, I hope she does. Maybe if everyone here is as nice as Anna seems, two weeks will be easier than I'm expecting.

"Adele?" she says. "Are you ready?"

I nod because saying yes would be a lie.

I follow behind her to the farthest cabin in the row. We stop on the steps, and she points to the door.

"Go ahead," she says. "Don't be shy."

I'm not shy. But I'm also not big on new people.

"You're not coming in?" I ask.

Anna smiles. "I'll open the door and let you in. But we think the campers should get to know each other on their own terms."

I swallow. I'm nervous. From inside the cabin, I can hear the voices of the other girls. But when we step into the room, everyone goes silent. There are four beds, and three of them are occupied by girls about my age. The first is a blond in a pink T-shirt. Her eyes are closed. The second is a girl with wispy brown hair and glasses. She's reading a thick book. The third camper, who has black hair in a pixie cut, is the only one who looks up.

"Ladies," says Anna. "This is Adele."

The girls answer in unison. "Hi, Adele."

"Introduce yourselves," Anna says. "And play nice, girls."

The counselor wags her finger at them and then she leaves. The room goes quiet. I shift from foot to foot. No one says anything or makes a move. I count to ten in my head. Then I throw my bag onto the only bed without sheets, and I wait.

Finally the black-haired girl stands up and walks over to me. She grins. She has braces and a nice smile. And her stomach is swollen out wide. When she sees me looking at it, she pats the roundness.

"Pregnant," she says.

"Are you sure you don't just have a watermelon under there?" I ask.

It's the worst joke I've ever made. But it makes the pregnant girl laugh.

"Oh god," she says. "I'm Sal. And I'm *so* glad to meet someone who isn't a dipshit."

The girl with the glasses giggles. The blond rolls her eyes and flips her ponytail. Then Sal flops herself onto my bed and makes introductions.

She jerks her thumb at the blond. "That's Lena." Then she points at the bookish one. "That's Liv."

"Adele," I reply.

"Yeah, we heard," says Lena.

"Dipshit," Sal whispers.

Right then I know who I'll be friendly with. And, more important, who I *won't* be friendly with.

It's the right call. For the next two days, I stick close to Sal. She's funny and she doesn't ask questions. The counselors keep us so busy that I don't have time to think about anything.

We swim and do archery. We take a day-long canoe trip.

Both nights, I fall asleep right away. I don't even dream.

The girls drop hints about why they're here. Liv is on her second drug-possession charge. Lena beat up a girl whose dad is a cop. And Sal did something she won't talk about. When they ask me about *my* stuff, I make a vague comment about shoplifting. Sal can sense my discomfort, and she changes the subject.

We don't talk about the boys next door, and it seems weird to me. A couple of times, I want to bring it up. But then I look at Sal's stomach and I don't do it.

I do see Andy once each day, when the boys are coming in for lunch and the girls are leaving. He flashes a charming smile at me both times. He puts a shiny apple on my tray. I thank him. I smile back. But I'm thinking about Fergus when I do it.

Why haven't I seen Fergus at all? Did he finish his book? What book *was* it? Did he cause trouble and get kicked out?

I tell myself I don't need to know. What I need is to take Andy's advice and put Fergus out of my mind. But knowing that doesn't stop me from trying to get an answer when I get a chance.

Chapter Four

It happens on the third night at Camp Happy. I'm pulled from a sound sleep by something. Maybe it's a sound. Maybe it's a feeling. Either way, my head is on the pillow one second, and the next, I'm sitting up.

For a moment all I do is blink. What woke me? My blood is rushing through my veins. And I look around the dark room, searching for an explanation. Nothing jumps out at me. The other girls are sleeping. Liv's mouth is open, and she's snoring lightly. Lena is buried under her blanket. Sal's arms and legs are spread wide, starfish style. It all looks normal. But my skin prickles.

I feel like I'm being watched.

My skin prickles harder. I wait another few seconds, listening. I don't hear anything. Just an owl in the distance. I count my own breaths, trying to calm my racing pulse. It doesn't work. The feeling of being watched doesn't leave. If anything, it gets stronger.

Careful to be extra quiet, I push my blanket off and put my feet on the floor. I shiver. The air in the cabin is so cool it's almost cold.

Did someone open the window?

I stand up and turn that way. And I almost scream. I have to clap my hands over my mouth to stop the noise.

Fergus is standing on the other side of the glass, and he's staring right at me. I can see him perfectly in the moonlight. His floppy hair. The bit of red at the front. His narrow shoulders. He's wearing a white tank top and plaid pajama pants. His eyes—which are green, I notice now—fix on me. He doesn't turn and run. He steps closer. In one hand he holds the same book I saw the other day. With the other hand, he makes a motion. *Come here,* it says.

I look back at the other girls. They haven't moved, but I pretend to study them. My heart is beating hard. Should I go to Fergus? Probably not. It's breaking the rules. If I believe Andy, it might even be a dangerous thing to do. But my feet move anyway.

When I get to the window, Fergus is right there. He's inches away. If not for the glass, I could reach out and touch him. The idea makes my skin get warm. I clench my hands into fists so I don't lift them up and embarrass myself.

I focus on his face. The darkness suits him, I decide. The shadows show off his features—his cheekbones and lips and perfect eyebrows. I see a tiny mole on the left side of his jaw. His nose, which is a bit crooked, has a small black stud in it. His lashes are long and full. Up close, his eyes seem even greener.

Part of my brain tells me I should stop staring. But a *bigger* part of my brain says that Fergus started staring first. He's the one who's standing outside the window of my cabin.

Does he like what he sees? Why do I care?

Like he can read my mind, Fergus smiles.

I want to blush. Hell. Maybe I *do* blush. But I also lift my chin and narrow my eyes, daring him to make this *my* problem. Then he surprises me. He drops a slow wink. His long lashes touch his cheek. A second passes, and he takes a step back. As I watch, he sets down his book on the windowsill. And he walks away.

"What the hell?" I say under my breath.

I stare down at the book. The spine is cracked, and there are no words on its black cover. There's nothing special about it at all. But when the breeze makes the pages flutter, I want to touch it. To hold it. To know what's inside of it.

I lift my eyes and peer into the night. Fergus is long gone. I don't know what he expects me to do. It's not like I can open the window to get the book. I can't risk waking up the other girls. Does he want me to come outside? That seems like a bad idea too.

I bite my lip. I glance at Liv, Lena and Sal. And I decide to start counting. If one of them opens her eyes before I get to ten, I'll stay. If not, I'll take it as a sign. But I only make it to six. Then my plans are changed by a flash of movement. It comes from outside the window, and my body starts moving right away.

Quickly and quietly I jog across the cabin floor. I hold my breath, unlock the door and open it. Then I step out. The air is chilly, and it rolls over me. But I ignore the cold. I look back and forth, trying to find the source of the flashing movement.

There!

I take a step. Then I stop so fast that I almost fall. Because while it *is* a person I see, it's not Fergus. The hair isn't dark enough. The body isn't lean and long enough.

Who is it?

My pulse spikes. I take a step backward. My body hits someone, and hands land on my arms. And for the second time tonight, I almost scream. The sound of my name keeps me quiet.

"Adele!" says Sal.

Shit.

I breathe out, and I turn to face her.

"What are you doing?" she asks.

"I just…heard something," I reply.

Her eyes flick a look around before she says, "What kind of something?"

"An owl maybe?"

"Well, if you go looking for every bird that comes around, you're going to get in trouble fast. Let's go back inside."

I start to nod. Then I remember the book.

"Hang on one sec," I say.

"What? Why?" replies Sal.

"I dropped something," I lie.

Avoiding her stare, I hurry to the other side of the cabin. The book is still there. I grab it. I flip it open, excited to see what's written inside. But what I see makes no sense to me.

Chapter Five

After I take the book and follow Sal back to our room, it's hard to fall asleep. What I saw, or didn't see, on the pages sticks in my brain. A hundred questions pop up too.

A blank book.

If Fergus had filled it with his own words, I would get it. Poems. Stories. Whatever. But *nothing*? It makes no sense.

When my eyes close, I see the empty pages of the book. Or I see Fergus's face and the wink he gave me. What's his deal?

A few times, I roll over in my bed and look at Sal. I think about waking her up. Maybe she knows something about Fergus and his story. But the truth is, I don't want to hear it from Sal. I want Fergus to tell me himself.

I toss and turn for the rest of the night. My sleep is so bad that it doesn't seem like sleep at all. When Sal wakes me up the next morning by tapping my arm, I feel like a zombie.

"Go away," I tell her.

"I can't," she says. "We're doing the rope course with the boys today. And we're late. Liv and Lena left, like, twenty minutes ago."

"You're going to climb ropes with that baby in you?" I ask.

"Nope," she replies. "I'm going to watch you and laugh."

I groan. I put the pillow over my face. I'd like to back out. I wonder if I can use my sore wrist as an excuse. But it's feeling a lot better. Plus I've been warned that not showing up equals a talk with the counselors. And I don't need that on my record. So I make myself get up and get dressed. I follow Sal out to the trees, where all the campers are getting ready to climb. Which is when I realize something. Fergus will be there.

I look for him while the counselors explain how the rope course works. My toes tingle as I think about seeing him. I imagine clever things to say. But it doesn't happen. There's zero sign of him.

Dammit.

"This sucks," I say.

"What sucks?" Sal replies.

"Nothing," I tell her. "But also…everything."

She laughs and then she pushes me closer to the rope course.

I'm tired. I'm slow. Once Andy has to help me get untangled. And I can't stop looking for Fergus. I don't see him. When I finish the course, I decide not to go a second time. I lie about my wrist bugging me. Then I flop to the ground and wait for Sal to show up again.

From my spot on the grass, I watch the other campers work the course. They're all smiling and giggling. It looks like fun. The real kind. Not just for show. For a second I let myself pretend this is a normal summer camp. One where my dad dropped me off. One where he told me he'll miss me. And one where he'll pick me up because he *wants* to rather than because the courts tell him he *has* to.

Suddenly my chest hurts. My eyes sting. Tears are coming.

I close my eyes and try to focus on something else. The way the sun warms my skin. A bird chirping somewhere close by. I start to relax. The need to cry fades. But then Lena ruins the moment.

"What's the matter, fat-ass?" she says. "Did a bit of exercise make you need a nap?"

I open my eyes. Lena is standing over me. She has makeup on today, probably because of the boys. Her lipstick-covered mouth is twisted in an ugly smile at the moment.

"If you want to insult me," I reply, "you'll have to try again. Even someone with a teeny tiny brain like yours can do better than *fat-ass*."

Lena's lips press together. I don't care. She's been trying hard to piss me off every day since I got to Camp Happy. I have no idea why. I've been ignoring her. But today her efforts annoy me. I sit up. I meet her glare.

"Why do you want to pick a fight with me, Lena? Am I that special?" I ask. "Or did someone make you sad when you were a little girl, and you can't let it go?"

"Shut up," she says.

I roll my eyes. "You came and talked to me."

Sal turns up then, and she gives Lena a dirty look before turning to me.

"Guess what day it is tomorrow?" she says.

"Uh...Friday?" I reply.

She nods. "That's right. And the counselors do a bonding thing after dinner on Fridays. We're pretty sure drinking is involved. A lot of drinking."

"Okay," I reply. "Why does that matter to me?"

"Not to you," says Sal. "To all of us."

Lena shakes her head. "I don't know why you're telling her. It's not like she's going to come. Or if she does, she'll just rat us out."

"What the hell makes you think I'm a rat?" I say.

"Because I think you're a goody-two-shoes," she tells me.

I shake my head. It seems stupid to point out that we're in a reform camp. The goody-goody factor is as close to zero as it can get. I look at Sal instead.

"We're going to sneak into the woods and have a bonfire," she says.

"That's—" I stop talking quickly as I remember that Lena *just* called me a goody-two-shoes. "That sounds fun."

"So you *do* want to come?" Sal asks.

Really, I *don't* want to. I want the days to stay filled with busy things. Things that don't involve getting kicked out of camp. But I can feel Lena staring at me. She's smug. As if she knows what I'm thinking. And I don't like it.

"Yeah, I'll come," I say.

Right after I speak, an unseen boy answers.

"You'll come where?" he asks.

For some reason, I know it's Fergus. I know that sounds weird. There's no way I can just know that. But I do anyway. So I'm not surprised at all when I turn and see him standing there.

He's got shorts on today. Cut-off jeans that come to his knees and show off his nice calves.

He's wearing a shirt for some band I've never heard of. There's a stack of leather bracelets on his left wrist, and a star tattoo on the right one. His face is dark. I see no trace of the smile from last night.

Fergus looks me in the eye and repeats his question. "You'll come where?"

"To the bonfire," I say.

"That's the worst fucking idea I've ever heard," he replies.

I blink. I open my mouth. But I don't get to answer. He spins on his heel and stalks off. He's moving so fast he almost crashes into another camper.

Lena, Sal and I are all silent. When Andy turns up a moment later and asks what's going on, Lena just leaves.

"Why does it seem like someone died?" Andy says.

Sal tells him about the bonfire, but she doesn't sound excited now.

"Is Fergus going?" Andy asks.

"It doesn't sound like it," I reply. "Why?"

"Because that would be a bad idea," he says.

He frowns and he looks in the direction Fergus has gone. Then Andy faces me again. He gives me a crooked smile. His blue eyes sparkle.

"I guess I better come to the bonfire too," he tells me. "Just to keep you out of trouble."

I think what he really means is that he wants to keep me safe from Fergus. But I'm not sure being protected is what I want.

What do *you want?* I ask myself.

I don't know the answer. But maybe tomorrow night's bonfire will give me a chance to figure it out.

Chapter Six

I assume the time before the bonfire is going to

pass slowly. But it doesn't.

The rest of the day goes by fast. We have a few

hours of free time. Sal makes me come with her

to the lake. The water is freezing, but she says

floating helps her back. From the dock I dangle

my toes in too. She tells me about the guy who

got her pregnant. He's older. Almost nineteen. An asshole who should never be a dad, Sal says. Of course, when she says "dad," I think about mine. I throw myself into the lake just to make my mind go somewhere else.

After dinner a guest speaker comes to camp. He throws out the same bullshit people like him always do. Stay in school. Respect yourself. Respect others. Get a job. Blah, blah. I don't buy it. And I don't think anyone else does either. The only good part of the speech is seeing Fergus.

The moment he walks into the room—late—I feel it. It's like my breath gets shorter. My heart goes a little faster. I pretend not to watch him. But I can see him from the corner of my eye. He sits alone. And unlike everyone else, he seems to be listening to the speaker. I stare at him for too long. Then Sal pokes me and asks what I'm doing, and I have to look away.

That night I sleep like the dead. No tossing and turning. No being woken up by Fergus outside my window.

And just like that, it's Friday night. I eat my last bite of pasta. Sal goes to the bathroom for the third time. I stack our dishes, and I hurry to put them in the bin. But Anna, the counselor, takes my tray before I can set it down.

"Adele Reimer," she says.

I look up, nervous. "Hi."

"How are things going?" she asks.

"Fine," I reply.

Anna smiles. I brace for her to say something I won't like. And she does. But it's not as bad as I think it will be.

"You've got dish duty tonight," she tells me. "You can meet the others in the back."

I breathe out. Then I go and break the bad news to Sal. She makes me promise to come to the fire after I'm done. I agree because I don't want her to be sad. And I take the hand-drawn map she gives me. But in my head, I'm asking if this is a sign. Maybe I shouldn't go to the fire. The whole time I'm washing the dishes, I think it. I swear I'm not going to go. But an hour later I'm in the dark woods. I've got the map in my hands. And I'm completely lost.

"Shit," I say.

I turn in a circle. There's nothing but trees and dirt. No hint as to which way to go.

"Double shit," I say.

I lift my eyes and look at the sky. It's clear. Stars dot the darkness. But I don't know how to use them to find my way.

I take a step. Then I stop because I hear something. A twig cracks. I get a fist ready, but I'm not going to run. If someone's going to attack me, I'm going to fight back. But a moment later, my fist drops. Fergus steps slowly out of the trees with his hands up.

"Don't hurt me," he says with a small smile. "You going to the fire?" he adds.

"That's the plan."

"Are you lost?"

I open my mouth. I'm going to lie. Fergus doesn't need to know the truth. It's embarrassing. But for some reason, at the last second I change my mind.

"Sal is bad at making maps," I say.

"Maps?" he says. "Let me see."

I hand him the little paper. Both of his nicely shaped eyebrows go up.

"This might *actually* be a map of the New York subway," he says.

I laugh. Fergus smiles at me. I notice that one of his bottom front teeth is crooked. It's nice that he's not perfect.

"Come on," he says. "I'll walk you there."

I put my hands on my hips. "Wait."

"What?"

"Are you going to kill me and bury me somewhere?"

"That got dark fast," he says.

"Well, you did tell me that going to the fire was the worst fucking idea in the world," I reply. "So your offer is a bit sus."

"Did my warning work?" he asks.

"No."

"Then I have to change *my* plan," Fergus says. "Let's go."

I like walking beside him. I like how his elbow bumps mine every couple of steps. And I *really* like it when he moves a prickly bush out of my way.

"Why were you reading a blank book?" I ask.

"No one can *read* a blank book," he says.

My face gets warm. But I don't let his statement stop me from answering.

"Fine. Why were you *pretending* to read a blank book?" I ask.

His mouth curves into that small smile again. "People talk to me less when I have a book open."

"Okay, then. Why use a fake book?"

"I like knowing something they don't know."

"You mean you like tricking people," I say.

"Yes, I do," he replies.

His honesty surprises me. It makes me go silent. For a few seconds the only sound is the crunch under our feet. Fergus is the one who speaks up next.

"People think I'm not very smart because I'm quiet," he says. "Or because I make bad choices. I like tricking them because they think it's not something I could do."

I nod. "I get it. When people hear even a bit about my life, they assume the worst."

I wait for Fergus to ask me for more details. He doesn't. I'd usually like that. I don't want to share pieces of my life. But tonight I almost wish he'd ask. I want him to be curious about me like I'm curious about him.

"So you don't read for real?" I want to know.

"Oh, I read," he says.

"Who's your favorite author, then?" I ask.

"Why?" he replies. "Do you think I'm lying?"

"Maybe. Maybe not," I joke.

He slows down. I can feel him getting tense. I think maybe I've offended him. I'm about to ask, but then I hear it. The other kids' voices. Laughing. Talking. Someone is even singing.

We take a few more steps, and the woods open into a clearing. Everyone is sitting around a crackling fire.

"Here's your subway stop," says Fergus.

His voice is kind of flat. Way different than it has been for the last few minutes. I frown. I look at the kids, trying to figure out why they make Fergus unhappy.

On the far side of the fire, Andy sees me and waves me over. My stomach dips. The bad feeling—the same one I had on my first day here—comes back.

I turn to Fergus. I'm going to ask if he wants to go somewhere else. But he's already taken off.

I scan the trees, looking for him. I even take a step. But Sal calls my name. And when I look toward her, I see Andy again. Now *his* eyes are on the forest. Is he trying to find Fergus too? Why do I feel like I have to stop him?

I smile a fake smile, and I move into the group.

Chapter Seven

As I sit down between Sal and Andy, I spot Lena. She's cross-legged on a flat rock, and she's giving me a death glare. I roll my eyes. What the hell is her problem?

"You good, babe?" says Sal.

"Yeah," I reply. "Dishes suck. And I got lost on the way in. But I'm here now."

She gives me a side hug. "And I'm so glad you are!"

I smile, and I swear to myself I won't look at Lena for the rest of the night. And it works. For a bit. Everyone is talking and having fun. Someone starts an old-school game of telephone. It's the one where a person whispers a sentence into someone's ear. Then that person whispers it to the next person. Our game starts on the other side of the fire. But it doesn't get to me. It ends at Sal.

Between giggles she yells out, "Every penis walks a dog!"

The kid who started the game yells back, "That's not what I said! Jesus, Sal, you perv!"

We all laugh then, and I never find out how the sentence started.

Andy tells a scary story. He grabs me at a tense moment. I scream. The laughs start all over.

We move on to a dirty-jokes contest. It gets bad fast.

Things settle down as the fire shrinks. After a bit a bottle gets passed around. When it comes my way, I can smell the booze wafting out of it. I think about taking a swig. I'm having a good time. What could it hurt? But I also think of my mom. And my dad. And for some reason, I think about the guest speaker from yesterday.

Make good choices. Those had been his last words before he left.

Pretty dorky. But it sticks in my head.

Some guy I don't know shakes the bottle at me.

"No, thanks," I say.

"More for me," he replies.

I smile. But the smile freezes on my face when I hear Lena's voice.

"What a surprise," she says. "The princess doesn't drink."

I look up. She's standing in front of me. Her eyes are glassy. She steps closer and grabs the bottle. She lifts it to her lips and takes a huge gulp. Then she meets my eyes and does it again.

"Have some," Lena says.

"I'm good," I reply.

"Yeah," she says. "*Too* good."

I shake my head. The whole campfire group is silent as they listen to us.

"I'm fine," I say. "Really. I just don't want a hangover."

Ignoring my words, she shoves the bottle into my face. Andy jumps in. His hand blocks Lena.

"Some of us don't need vodka to have fun," he says.

Lena stops moving. She lets Andy take the bottle away. She even smiles. And when I see the way she looks at him, I realize something. She likes him. Which means she *doesn't* like it when he talks to me. And it must be why she's been so nasty all week.

I want to groan. Andy is hot. Model hot. He's also been super nice. But I have zero interest in him. Not like that. If I could, I'd just tell Lena so right now. If I thought she wouldn't freak out. She's swaying on her feet and giving me a drunk glare. The air around me suddenly feels tight. The smoke is bugging my throat too. I need some space and I need it fast.

"I'll be back in a bit," I say, standing up as I speak.

"You all right?" Sal asks.

I nod and tell an easy lie. "Just need to pee."

"Don't let a bear bite your ass," she says.

"I'll do my best," I promise.

I feel better as soon as I'm away from the crowd. I keep walking until I find a tree with a wide trunk, and I lean against it. I close my eyes and take a slow breath. The cold from the tree seeps into my back. It's nice. And, better still, a bit of wind kicks up and muffles the sounds from the fire. I breathe again. In and out. It takes five minutes, but I finally feel okay. Just as I decide to go back to the fire, I stop again. Because I can hear yelling.

My body goes still. My ears are on alert. And yep. There's a lot of yelling. But it's the mad kind, not the scared kind. I hear Anna's voice, and I figure out what's going on.

The counselors have busted us.

"Oh, shit," I say. "Shit, shit, *shit.*"

My pulse is sky-high. This can't happen. My dad can't find out about this. He already has too many reasons to not want me. My past. My probation. The reform camp on its own. Add this too? Not a chance. But as I stand there in a panic, I clue in. They've busted everyone else. But they haven't busted *me.* Not yet.

I look around. Is there an easy way out? Can I make it back to camp without being found? I don't know. But I can try. Maybe I won't get as lost on the way back.

I move away from the tree. When I do, I gasp. A pair of green eyes is peering out from the trees.

Fergus.

He's on a log. His knees are bent, so he's as short as me. He shakes his head, short and quick.

I understand what he's saying. *Keep quiet.*

I nod, and he hops down. His boots make nearly no noise when they hit the dirt.

He jerks his head to the side. *Follow me.*

I do. I stick close to his back. But I'm not as good at hiking in the dark as he is, and I trip twice. On my third near fall, Fergus turns and takes my hand. I'm surprised. But his fingers are warm and nice. I don't want to pull away, so I don't try. In fact, it might be the best thing that's happened at Camp Happy. And I want to hold on as long as I can.

Chapter Eight

By the time Fergus slows down, I'm a little out of breath. Maybe a *lot* out of breath, if I'm telling the truth. And that's probably the reason I don't notice until then that we've been moving farther into the woods. It's darker. Quieter. And when I speak, my whisper sounds way too loud.

"Are we going the wrong way?" I ask.

"No," says Fergus. "When the counselors look around, they'll look close to camp. This will give us time before they search the cabins too."

"Shit," I reply. "What if we don't get back first?"

"Then you can just tell them what you told Sal."

"What did I tell Sal?" I ask.

"That you had to use the bathroom," he replies.

My face heats up. "Are you stalking me, or what?"

"Maybe," he says. "But just a tiny bit."

"Very funny."

"Maybe I wanted to make sure you didn't get ax-murdered."

"You know...for a guy who's worried about ax murders," I say, "you spend a weird amount of time skulking in the woods."

"And for a girl at a camp for bad kids, you're pretty worried about being good," he replies. "I saw you refuse the vodka."

"Great. Now you sound like Lena."

"Ouch," he says. "I'm insulted."

"Ditto," I reply.

We both laugh, and it feels extra normal. Like we aren't two kids at a camp for criminals. And then I go and spoil the moment.

"My mom's an addict," I say.

Now my face isn't just warm. It's burning. But Fergus doesn't seem bothered by my blurted words.

"Oh yeah?" he replies. "Is that why you didn't want a drink?"

I shrug. "I don't know. All my mom's shitty choices seem to happen when she drinks or gets high, so…"

"I get it," he tells me. "My mom is dead. But when she was alive, her favorite poison was meth."

I nod. But I don't say I'm sorry. People always say they're sorry when someone dies. I can't stand to be a cliché. We keep walking. Fergus hasn't let go of my hand. And in the silent moment I notice a rough patch on his palm. Without thinking about it, I put my thumb between our hands and rub the spot.

"What happened here?" I ask.

I kind of regret the question when he pulls his fingers free. He stops and holds out his palm. The puckered scar is silver in the moonlight.

"I cut it breaking a window," he says.

"On purpose?" I reply.

"Well, I broke the window on purpose," he tells me. "The cut was a mistake."

I roll my eyes, and he grins. I note his crooked tooth again. I like it even more this time.

"What about you?" he asks.

I'm not sure why, but I know he's wondering about *my* scars. I take a small step back. I grab the bottom of my shirt and pull it up to my bellybutton. Fergus's gaze drops. I don't feel nervous. I close my eyes. I don't have to look. I know what he can see. I've got a white line running all the way across my stomach. It's jagged. Ugly. The biggest reason I never wear a bikini or a crop top.

"How old were you?" Fergus asks.

His voice is down near my scar, and I open my eyes. He's bent over. When he breathes out, I can feel it on my stomach. Goose bumps pop up everywhere. I have to swallow before I answer Fergus.

"I was eight," I say.

I tell him the rest of the story. My mom, as messed up as ever. The fight she'd had with her boyfriend of the moment. I'd wanted a sandwich. Instead I'd gotten a glass-topped table flipped at me. And no hospital after. Because a hospital would've meant having to tell someone what happened. My mom's boyfriend sealed my injury with glue. When I'm done talking, I'm tired. But I'm weirdly lighter too. I've never told anyone the story before. It's kind of good to have it out there in the open.

"Jesus," says Fergus. "That's fucking awful."

"Oh, you think?" I say.

He stands up and says, "Glad you made it out alive."

His green eyes are serious. Intense too. I feel a blush creeping up.

"It's not the worst thing I've had to put up with," I reply.

He doesn't ask for more details. And for the second time, I half wish he would. I don't even know why I want to tell him things. I never want to tell anyone things. But the way Fergus is looking at me makes me want to confess every detail of my life. I have to bite my lip to stop the words from bursting out.

"Guess I get why you don't drink," he says.

"What about you?" I ask.

He doesn't answer. Not right away. He just lifts his own shirt. I suck in a startled breath. My scar is bad. But what he's showing me now is really, *really* bad.

Fergus's entire chest is covered in a lacy pattern. The scars are raised and purple. They're healed, but they still look fresher than mine.

"I don't drink," he says. "Not anymore."

I listen as he tells me his story. Two years ago he and a friend had been drinking in his basement. A fire broke out upstairs. He and his friend escaped, but Fergus's mom was still inside. He ran back in to save her.

"I failed," he says.

My heart hurts. It's a burn in my chest. I can't think of anything to say. Now *I'm sorry* wouldn't be cliché—it would be useless. I want to throw my arms around him. Maybe I would even do it, but we've started walking again.

"I ask myself all the time if it'd be different if I'd been sober," Fergus says. "Like, what if I'd had thirty extra seconds? My mom was high as shit. But is that what mattered?"

I reach out and take his hand. His fingers get tight on mine right away.

"I give zero out of five stars to running into a burning building," he tells me. "In case you were wondering."

"No shit," I reply.

I'm going to say more, but I look up and see we've circled back to the cabins. We're still in the trees, but the red roofs are just in sight. And it happened way too fast. I don't want to go in. I don't want my time with Fergus to be over. But being close to camp reminds me that we could still get busted. My need to stop that from happening is strong.

"Thank you," I say.

"For what?" Fergus says.

"For making sure I got to the fire tonight," I tell him. "And for making sure I got back from it too."

He shrugs. "To tell you the truth, it was kind of selfish."

"What do you mean?" I ask.

His hand comes up to my cheek. His palm curves against my skin. The touch is warm, and a tingle moves over my whole body.

He asks a silent question. *Is this okay?*

I nod my consent. *Yes, please.*

I close my eyes. I shift my weight forward and tip up my face. And a heartbeat later, Fergus's lips are on mine. The cabins don't exist. The camp doesn't exist. There's just him and me. There's just *us*.

Chapter Nine

I've kissed before. I've *been* kissed before. More than once.

There was my friend Leo when I was five, and Tommy Santos in eighth grade. I played spin the bottle at a party when I was fourteen. Two years ago I had a really gross make-out session with Hendrix Earl. He tasted like bad cheese. And just a few months ago, there was Farley Jenkins. He was my boyfriend. Until he met my mom and couldn't handle it. But none of them kissed me like this. None of them made me understand what *toe-curling* means. Right now, with Fergus's mouth on mine, it makes total sense. I want to melt.

My heart beats hard.

My stomach flips.

My legs are wobbly.

My toes 100 percent want to curl up in my boots.

And when he lets go, I immediately want to kiss him again. Hell. I'd even ask him to, but my brain isn't working. All I can do is stare at him. At his green eyes. At his not-perfect smile. I'd feel kind of stupid if he wasn't staring at me the same way.

"Hey," he says after a second.

"Hey," I say back.

He rocks on his heels. Then he swipes his hand over his mouth like he's trying to cover his grin. It makes my heart speed up again.

"I have to go," he tells me.

"I know," I reply.

"I don't want to."

I smile. "*I* don't want you to."

His smile is even bigger than mine. "Night, Adele."

"Night, Fergus."

I turn and walk a few steps. But I stop almost right away. I touch my lip, and I spin back around. Fergus hasn't moved. It would make me smile again if I weren't about to say something serious.

"You all right?" he asks.

I answer quickly so I don't chicken out. "There's another reason I didn't want to drink tonight. And it might sound silly, and I don't want you to judge me, but I just want you to know, okay? It's my dad. He's been gone for a long time. Ten years maybe." I pause to take a breath, but I don't stop. "He didn't leave because of me. It was my mom's shit. He got clean. She didn't. She used me to get to him. To get his money. For drugs. And now she's in rehab. My dad *has* to come back for me, so…" I trail off and shrug.

"And you don't want him to think you're like her," says Fergus.

"Yes," I reply. "I don't want to make any bad moves. Because if he changes his mind, I have nowhere to go."

I search his face. I'm not sure what I'm looking for. Maybe a sign that I've said too much. But Fergus's eyes are soft. He gets it. I can tell.

For the second time, he steps in and touches my cheek. The toe-curling feeling sweeps in. But before I can get the kiss I want, there's a crash. We both jump. We turn toward the sound. It came from the camp.

"Guess we need to hurry," Fergus says.

"Dammit," I say.

He laughs, then brushes his lips over mine.

"You go first," he says. "I'll wait and keep an eye out for ax murderers."

I make a face and then I take off. I look back a couple of times. Fergus is in the same spot every time. It's not until I get to my cabin that he's gone. I'm sad for a heartbeat. Then I remember that I'll get to see him again tomorrow.

A good reason to get to sleep fast.

Slowly I open the door. I inhale and hold the air in my lungs. I'm ready for a hundred questions if anyone *is* awake. But when I step inside, the other beds are empty. I frown. I don't want to see Lena. It doesn't matter too much if I see Liv. But a girlie moment with Sal wouldn't be so bad.

Where are they?

I step over and look out the window. The only signs of life are at the counselors' cabin. And I don't think that's a good thing. I feel a bit guilty, but not so much that I'm going to turn myself in.

Instead I climb into bed and pull the blanket over my chin.

I think about Fergus. About kissing him. About telling him things I never tell anyone. I smile and drift off, full of warm thoughts. And the next thing I know, the morning sun is pulling me from sleep.

I rub my eyes, sit up and look for the other girls. But they're still missing. I can see their beds haven't been slept in.

"Shit," I say. "What the hell happened?"

I swing my feet to the floor, and I quickly get dressed and head outside. It's quiet. I let myself steal a look at Fergus's cabin. It's quiet too.

Puzzled, I make my way down to the mess hall for breakfast. It's a bit louder inside. But it's not as noisy as it has been.

I scan the room for Sal. For Liv. Even for Lena. I don't see them. In fact, a few kids are missing. And I'm pretty sure they're the ones who were at the fire. I glance around for someone who might know where the others are. No one looks up from their food. After a second I give up. I grab a piece of toast, and I leave.

Walking around the camp alone is weird. I keep thinking someone is going to catch me and accuse me of doing something wrong. No one does.

For what seems like a long while, I don't even see anyone else. But finally I hear sounds coming from near the trees. I follow the noise. And I find them. My roommates. Some other campers. Girls and boys. They're all wearing plastic gloves. And they're holding bags and buckets.

Garbage duty, I realize.

It must be their punishment.

And, of course, it's Lena who sees me first.

"Princess," she says. "So nice of you to join us."

I try to answer. "I'm not—"

She interrupts me. "Joining us? Oh, I *know* you're not. We *all* know you're not."

"What's that supposed to mean?" I ask.

"It means you're a rat. Just like I said."

I start to deny it. But I don't get the chance. Because Lena pulls off one of her gloves and aims her fist at my face.

Chapter Ten

I duck just in time. Lena's fist flies over my head instead of into it. But her swing is hard. And when she misses me, she falls forward. Her chin smacks the ground. She snarls, pushes up and spits out a mouthful of dirt.

"You little bitch!" she yells. "You knocked me down!"

I step back and say, "You fell over because you were trying to hit me. I don't think *I'm* the bitch here."

In reply, she jumps at me again. And again I manage to get out of her way.

The other kids have stopped what they're doing and are all watching us.

"You are a bitch," Lena snaps. "A rat *and* a bitch. A dirty, bitchy rat."

"I don't want to fight you," I say.

"Chickenshit," she says.

She comes at me, and now I don't duck or sidestep. I put my arm out and my hand up. Lena runs right into my palm. She stumbles backward and almost falls again.

Where are the counselors?

But I don't dare ask. I can't even look around for them. It will just give people even more reason to think I'm a rat.

And Lena isn't done with her attack. She wipes her mouth. She fixes a glare my way. And she lunges. I try to avoid her. But this time I'm a bit too slow. One of Lena's hands clips my shoulder. The hit isn't hard, but it still sends me off-balance. Lena sees it. She dives in once more. She tries to grab my hair, and her nails scrape the side of my neck. The sting finally makes me want to fight back. I clench a fist. But I don't get to swing it. Warm hands grab my elbows and pull me away. I know it's Fergus even before his voice fills my ear.

"Think about your dad," he says.

His words make me drop my fist.

"Chickenshit," Lena repeats.

"Get the hell out of here before you get all of us into even more trouble," Fergus says to her.

She spits again. But she also listens. And not a second too soon. As Lena slips away, two counselors show up. One is Anna. The other is a man whose name I can't remember.

"Everything okay?" Anna asks.

Sal is quick to answer, her voice cheery. "All good!"

The male counselor frowns at Fergus. "Are you supposed to be on this work crew, Mr. Malone?"

"No, sir," says Fergus. "Just passing by."

"Get going then," the counselor replies.

"Yes, sir."

Fergus looks at me, sending one of his silent messages. *See you later.*

I nod. But when he leaves, I'm ready to follow right then. I *want* to follow. I even expect to be kicked out next. But Sal grabs my arm and pulls me closer, and no one says a word to me. A couple more seconds pass, and the two counselors go back to wherever they came from.

"I should get out of here," I say to Sal.

She shakes her head. "No way. Lena is probably waiting for you. And besides that, my back is killing me, and the baby is sitting on my bladder. You have to help me finish."

She throws a fresh pair of gloves at me, and I catch them in the air. I have zero interest in garbage duty. But I have even less interest in arguing. And she's right. Lena probably *is* waiting for me. And she might have something scarier than a fist this time.

"I don't know what the hell her problem is," I mutter.

"Well, for one, she thinks you told on us," says Sal.

"Yeah, I got that bit," I reply. "I just don't know *why* she thinks that."

"You're the only one who didn't get busted, dummy."

"Because I wasn't at the fire when the bust happened."

"I know that," Sal replies. "And *you* know that. But what *we* know doesn't matter."

"Lena knows it too," I say. "Everyone at the stupid fire saw me leave."

"Yeah, but Lena is telling everyone you left at *just* the right moment."

"I did leave at the right moment. I got lucky, that's all." I bend down and pick up a candy wrapper. "Where does all this garbage come from?"

"Um...from slack-ass, good-for-nothing teens like you and me," says Sal. "Duh. They run this reform camp ten months of the year."

"That's a lot of slack-ass, good-for-nothing teens," I reply.

"No shit."

We're both quiet for a minute or two. Or I'm quiet, anyway. Sal grunts and groans about her back. My mind returns to Fergus. Clearly, he heard everything I said last night. Understood it too. Bringing up my dad like he did shows it.

And on the subject of Dad…

I still have another week of this to finish. I can't get in fights. I should avoid anything that puts me on the counselors' radar.

"Hey," says Sal. "Did you hear about Andy?"

"No," I reply, snapping out of my thoughts. "Why? Didn't he get garbage duty too?"

"Worse, probably," she states. "This is, like, his third strike or something."

"Aren't we all on our third strike? Isn't that the point?"

"Third strike at Camp Happy."

"Hang on. You mean Andy's been here before?" I ask.

Sal nods. "Tons of kids do it instead of whatever else. But you only get three chances, so you can't fuck it up that many times."

"But Andy seems so…" I trail off, then shrug. "*Good.*"

"Oh, please," says Sal. "No one *that* good winds

up at Camp Happy. He's done things you don't want to know about, for sure. But anyway. It means Andy's probably kicked out."

"Shit."

"Yeah."

I pick up a piece of random plastic. As I toss it into Sal's bucket, someone clears their throat behind me. I turn, hoping to find Fergus. But it's Andy. Did he hear everything we just said? My skin warms with embarrassment. If he did hear, he doesn't say. He just gives me one of his charming smiles.

"Can I talk to you?" he asks. "Alone?"

I look at Sal. She shrugs. But I hold back.

"Adele?" says Andy.

I make myself nod. "Sure. But just for a minute, okay? I don't want to get in trouble."

As I follow him to a spot in the trees, my palms are sweaty inside my gloves. I think of Fergus and his ax-murderer jokes. And I think of what Sal just told me about Andy's three strikes.

"What's up?" I ask.

"I didn't get to say goodbye to you last night," Andy replies. "You left before we got shut down."

"Good timing," I say. "What about you?"

"*My* timing is terrible," he jokes.

Right after he says it, he leans in a bit. I realize he's about to try to kiss me. I take a quick step back.

"What did you want to talk to me about?" I ask.

Andy's charming smile is gone. He fixes me with a cold look. And my palms get even sweatier.

"I wanted to give you some more advice," he says.

"Okay."

"If you want to stay alive, you should ask Fergus why he's really here."

His words make the air around me feel colder. So cold that I kind of freeze in place. And when he strides away, all I can do is stand there and stare.

Chapter Eleven

Sal and I finish up garbage duty and head back to camp. She leaves to check in with the counselors and grab a shower. I pick up Fergus's blank book and pretend to read. But I'm really just waiting until she's gone so that I can search for Fergus.

I check the whole camp. The mess hall. The rope course. The dock, the basketball court and the archery range. I even sneak a look into his cabin's window. He's nowhere.

It's past lunch by the time I give up. But I'm starving, so I grab a sandwich from the kitchen and make my way to my cabin to eat. Lena and Liv aren't there. But I find Sal on her bed, eating cookies straight from the package.

"Don't judge me," she says as I walk in. "And you look like hell."

I give her a tired eyeroll. "Gee, thanks."

"Where've you been? I could've given birth in the time you've been gone."

I start to lie. But I change my mind. I sigh and tell her I was looking for Fergus and why. And she responds with a funny look.

"Okay, that doesn't make any sense," she says.

"Why not?" I ask.

She flops back against her pillow. "Because why would Andy tell you to ask Fergus why he's here?

They're at Camp Happy for the same reason."

"I still don't get it," I say.

"They were friends. Like, besties. Or whatever boys call it when they're besties."

My skin prickles. And I know what's coming next before Sal speaks again.

"They got drunk one night," she says. "They did some messed-up shit together."

"The night Fergus's house burned down?" I ask.

She nods and says, "You mean the night *Fergus* burned it down?" Her words make me feel even colder than Andy's did earlier. I'm not even sure I heard her right. I stare at her.

"I don't understand," I tell her.

"Fergus and Andy got drunk." Sal says it slowly. "They lit a fire. It burned down."

"But Fergus's mom *died* in that fire," I say.

"Exactly. Then Fergus was in the hospital. Andy was in juvie. And they both got sent here. I told you before that you didn't want to know, didn't I?"

The room spins. I feel like I'm underwater.

"Adele?" says Sal. "Are you okay?"

I blink, and the room comes into focus again. I need to be sure she's right.

"How do you know all this?" I ask.

"Liv told me," she replies.

"Liv?" I echo.

"Sleeps in our room. Quiet. Brown hair. Glasses."

I give her a dirty look. "I know who she is. I just can't imagine her talking for more than ten seconds at a time."

"She told me," Sal says. "Cross my heart, hope to die and all that shit."

"But how did—" I stop myself mid-sentence. "Never mind. It doesn't matter how she found out, does it?"

A million thoughts are running around in my head. But one is bigger than the rest.

Did Fergus lie to me?

A hollow feeling forms in my chest. *Why* would

he lie? Weirdly, it's Andy's voice that answers in my head.

Because he's bad news. He lied because he wanted to kiss you. More than kiss you. I tried to warn you.

"Shut up," I mutter.

"Hey!" says Sal. "I didn't say anything!"

I don't answer her. I step toward the door.

"Where are you going?" Sal asks.

"Where do you think?" I say.

Sal shakes her head. "Uh-uh. You can't go looking for Fergus right now."

"I have to."

"No, you have to go to the mandatory group-therapy session."

"I don't want a useless therapy session," I say.

"We're not allowed to miss it," Sal replies.

"I don't care!" I almost yell.

"Jesus, you're worked up," says Sal. "Why do you care so much what Fergus—ohhhh. You *like* him."

I don't deny it. I do like him. Of course I like him. Which is why it hurts so much to realize he might've lied to me.

"You can find him later," Sal promises. "I'll help you."

I nod. I thank her. But we don't find him. In fact, the rest of the day is nothing but frustration. The therapy session sucks. The counselor running it gets annoyed at me for not speaking up. One of the other campers pukes, and it gets on my shoes. And things don't get better.

We're forced to play capture the flag. Fergus doesn't show.

Dinner is the worst meatloaf in the world. No Fergus.

A girls-only night hike rounds things off. And clearly, Fergus doesn't come to that.

At lights-out, Lena gives me the silent treatment until she goes to bed. Liv passes out with her book in her face. Sal is the last to stay awake other than me, but she still drifts off way before I'm able to. And when I'm *finally* sleepy, a thump from outside jerks me awake again. I'm pissed off for a second. Then I remember the last time I got woken up at night.

Fergus. The book.

Quickly I roll over and stand up. I barely look at the other girls, and I don't bother checking the window. I just head right out the door. And while I don't see Fergus right away, I do see someone who could be him. A figure is hurrying between the cabins on the boys' side.

Should I follow him?

I don't even wait to answer myself. If it *is* Fergus, I don't want to lose this chance. If it *isn't* Fergus, then no big deal.

But I don't get far. Only four or five steps. I'm stopped by a bang. Not the gunshot kind. The explosion kind. Like a firecracker. A really *big* firecracker.

With my heart slamming at double speed, I spin toward the noise. And it's easy to see the source of the sound. Smoke is pouring from one of the cabins.

Not just one of the cabins, I realize.

It's Fergus's cabin.

Chapter Twelve

The smell of fire cuts through the air. There's silence. Then a yell comes from inside the cabin. A heartbeat passes. One boy comes stumbling out. The smoke follows him in a huge puff. A few seconds pass. Two other boys exit the building too. They're moving more slowly than the first. One is helping the other, who looks hurt. The smog is already so thick that I can't tell if any of them is Fergus.

I know I should get closer. I should be screaming for help. I should be *giving* help. But my feet refuse to go anywhere.

One of the boys sinks to the ground. My heart drops with him.

Not Fergus, I realize. Too short.

An alarm blares. It's a bit late. But at least the high-pitched sound makes my body unfreeze.

My bare feet slap the ground as I hurry toward the boys. I'm not the only person running now. Other campers are coming too. By the time I get to the smoking cabin, a counselor is tearing down the path. She has a red fire extinguisher in one hand and a flashlight in the other. And she doesn't stop when she reaches the cabin. She runs right in.

One of the boys—the one who came out first—coughs and says, "There's no one in there."

A male counselor is at his side, and he repeats the boy's words in a yell. The woman who ran into the cabin runs out again. She stops beside her co-worker.

I can't hear what they say to each other. Something about a pipe bomb. Something else about less damage than expected.

But I'm distracted. And not just because I still haven't spotted Fergus. I see now that the injured boy is Andy. Gray soot covers his face and clothes. He has a red slash on one of his cheeks. It all makes my throat dry, and I'm scared to think about why that might be.

"Come on," says the counselor with the fire extinguisher. "Let's get Andy up to the first-aid room."

"I'll stay down here and ask some questions," says another one.

Anna is there too. She turns to the rest of us.

"Okay, everyone!" she calls out. "Back to your cabins! We'll be by to check on each and every one of you very shortly!"

The other campers do as they've been asked to do. But I stick around. I hear someone say that Fergus wasn't in the cabin with his roommates. He's still unaccounted for. And I still want the same thing I've wanted all day—to know where he's gone.

I slip in behind the smoking cabin and wait. I'm kind of expecting him to just show up. He doesn't. I'd like to stay there until he does, but I can't. The counselors are looking around now, and I don't want to risk getting found. So I have no choice but to head back to my own cabin.

Time passes fast and slow at the same time.

Anna comes and asks her questions. I don't tell her I was already outside when the explosion happened.

Liv, Lena and Sal go back to sleep.

I lie awake, thinking about Fergus. My stomach won't stop churning. My eyes are sticky with tiredness, but I can't seem to pass out.

An hour passes. Then another.

I roll over and stare at the wall. Before long the sun will come up. And then what?

After a little bit more time, I hear voices outside the cabin. It's the counselors. I don't mean to listen to them. Really. But I can't help it. They're talking about Fergus. He's still gone. And with his history involving fire, they have questions. They're going to call the police. A park ranger is on his way already.

I want to jump out and argue with them. It's one thing to think he lied to me, but it's a whole other to think he'd set a bomb. And no matter what, I just can't believe Fergus would do this. He wouldn't hurt someone on purpose. It's not fair for the counselors to use his past against him. The whole point of Camp Happy is to move forward.

I have to find him.

But a second later I change my mind. I don't just have to find him. I have to prove he's innocent.

Because he's not guilty. Every bit of me knows it. And knowing it means I have to ask an important question.

Why isn't he coming forward to say it?

I don't know. But it's just another reason to look for him.

It's risky to sneak out, but I do it anyway. I tiptoe back to Fergus's cabin and look around. But it's really dark. And, unlike on the bonfire night, the moon isn't out. Clouds block the stars. I'm about to give up when I see something on the ground near my feet. It's half-covered by a leaf. But it shimmers a bit, even in the dim light. I feel a weird prickle on the back of my neck.

What is it?

I look back and forth. When I'm sure no one is watching, I bend down. As I do, a smell wafts up. Gasoline. Or something close. My nose wrinkles. But I grab the shiny thing anyway. When I pick it up, I see that it's a watch. It has a wide face, no numbers and a leather strap. And it's familiar. It only takes me a second to figure out why. This is the watch I saw on Andy's wrist the day I got to camp.

It must've fallen off when they helped him go to first aid.

But the prickle on my neck stays. The gas smell is even stronger now that the watch is in my hand. I stare down at it. And it hits me. The watch is clean. There's no soot. No damage. No sign of being near the explosion or the fire.

It could mean nothing. But my gut says it means everything.

I squeeze the watch. I take a moment to calm my racing heart. And I spin toward the counselors' cabins, determined to get help. Except I don't get that far.

The dirt crunches behind me. It's the only warning I have. Then something solid smashes into the back of my head. Pain bursts through my skull. And the world goes black.

Chapter Thirteen

I wake up suddenly. I'm out. Then I'm not.

A moldy smell fills my nose. My head is throbbing so badly that I can't open my eyes. I feel like I need to puke. But I *can't* puke. Because something is blocking my mouth.

I'm gagged, I realize. And tied up too.

Fear overtakes the sick feeling. I force my eyes open. It's dark where I am. I can't see much. But a few things come into focus. I'm lying on my side on a mattress. Wire is wrapped around my wrists, and a skinny piece of cloth is around my ankles.

I try to groan. The gag blocks the sound. Panic slides through me, but I tell myself not to give in to it.

I close my eyes again. I have to work hard at not freaking out. I need to be calm if I want to get out of this.

Whatever this *is*, says a little voice in my head.

Silently I tell it to shut the hell up and then I count to ten. Then twenty. I get to thirty-three before I'm ready to look again.

It's still dark. It's still scary. But I'm more in control now. I wiggle myself up to a seated position and try to figure out where I am.

The walls are wood. And they remind me of my cabin at Camp Happy. I blink a few times and decide this *is* a cabin. Clearly it can't be one of the ones inside the camp. But it's a lot like them. And it feels good to know at least a small something.

What else?

My eyes are getting used to the dark. I take a wider look around. And right away I find something that makes my pulse jump. There's someone else in the room. A huddled form on the floor. One I know.

Oh god. Oh shit.

It's Fergus. And he's very still.

I try to say his name. Of course, the gag stops me. I make a frustrated noise and push at the cloth with my tongue. It takes a lot of effort, but I manage to spit it out.

"Fergus!" I call.

He doesn't answer.

"Fergus!" I say it louder this time.

He doesn't even move.

Please don't let him be dead.

"Fergus!" I repeat.

He still doesn't reply. But his hand shifts from the ground to his hip.

"Oh, thank god," I say.

My relief only lasts for a minute. When I try to shuffle off the bed, the cabin door opens. Light comes in. And so does Andy. Without meaning to, I cringe back against the wall.

"You're awake," says Andy.

"Sorry to let you down," I reply.

"Have you tried screaming yet?" he asks. "If not, don't bother. We're too far away from camp for anyone to hear you."

I don't know if I believe him. But his face is relaxed. If he's lying, he's really good at it.

"Where are we?" I ask. "You can't have taken us *that* far."

Andy flashes one of his charming smiles. "You should never doubt the power of a good wheelbarrow." He sweeps his hand over the room.

"Welcome to the *old* Camp Happy. Not too far from the new one. But far enough."

He steps fully into the cabin. The door closes behind him, and the darkness gets thicker again. My heart thumps.

"You need to let us go, Andy," I say.

"I can't," he tells me.

He moves across the room. He's got some kind of container in his hands. I can hear liquid sloshing around inside it.

It's a gas can, I realize.

I fight a gasp.

"If it makes you feel better, I'm sorry," Andy says. "I didn't want to involve you. And I did try to warn you to stay away from Fergus."

I hold back a need to look at Fergus's still body. I use my calmest voice to reply. In fact, I talk in the voice my social worker uses. Kind. Patient. And like I mean it.

"I know you warned me," I say. "But I don't get it."

"I was a good kid," Andy states. "Straight fucking As. Good fucking family. Nice shit everywhere. Then I met Fergus. He needs to be punished for what he took from me."

"He lost his mom, Andy," I say.

"His mom was a druggie bitch," he replies. "He's better off without her. That fire did him a favor. This one won't."

I press my teeth together. I don't tell him my mom was an addict too. I don't say that addiction is a disease, even though it is.

Instead I test the strength of the wire holding me. I rub my wrists together and pull them apart. They get a tiny bit looser. I try harder. And I talk so Andy doesn't see what I'm doing.

"You can't just kill us," I say. "They'll figure it out."

"But *I'm* not killing you," he replies. "Fergus is. He's got a thing for fire. They already believe he set off the bomb at our cabin. They'll believe he did this too."

He unscrews the cap on the gas can. His movement isn't hurried. It isn't slow either. It's just…casual. And it's the same when he starts tossing the gasoline around the cabin.

He's really going to do this.

I don't have time to get myself free. The place will burn down before I can manage. My only choice is to do something now, and the only option I see is to throw myself at him. So that's what I do.

Fighting the ache in my head, I push up from the bed. I hurl my whole body toward Andy. And it works. I surprise him. He stumbles, and he falls back. I land on top of him, but it doesn't matter. His head hits the wood floor hard. His eyes close, and he doesn't move.

The gas can lands beside us, the liquid spilling out. The smell makes me gag.

I roll away from Andy. The fall snapped the wire on my wrists, and I want to cry with relief. But I turn toward Fergus instead. And I want to cry again. His eyes are open. He looks confused, but he's awake and moving.

"Adele?" he says.

"We have to get out of here."

Quickly I untie my legs. Then I move over to Fergus and get to work on the rope around his ankles and wrists. It takes a minute, but I get it done. I look up as I finish. And my heart just about stops. Andy has woken up. He has a match in his hand. And he's getting ready to light it.

Chapter Fourteen

For a second time, I think my only choice is to hurl myself at Andy. But I'm not fast enough. He strikes the match on the floor. It sparks. The tiny flame flickers. And then he tosses it toward the gasoline, and all hell breaks loose.

A whooshing noise fills the air. The gas ignites in blue and orange. The flames come quick and strong, and sour smoke is there right away too.

Fear freezes me. But Fergus grabs my arm. He pulls me to my feet. Together, we stumble toward the door. As we exit, I look back. Andy's eyes are closed again.

Oh, shit.

I try to say something to Fergus, but I choke on the smoke. The words don't come out. I suck in a breath of fresher air. I choke on it too. Tears pour down my cheeks, and it takes a few seconds for me to catch my breath. In that short amount of time, the cabin lights up. The dry wood and the gasoline make it happen fast.

"You okay?" Fergus asks.

I manage a nod. He nods back. Then he bolts back to the cabin.

He's going to save Andy, I realize.

I squeeze my hands into tight fists. Fergus is willing to risk his own life to help someone who tried to kill him. If I weren't so scared for him,

I'd be worried about liking him even more than I already do.

Hurry, hurry!

And a moment later, he bursts out again. He's got Andy under his arm. Fergus drags him away from the burning building and drops him to the ground.

Overhead a helicopter whirs. I look up. A chopper is circling closer. And the sun is just starting to rise behind it. The horizon is the same color as the fire eating away at the cabin.

The counselors come rushing in then, and for the next couple of hours, everything is a blur. There are cops. Firefighters. Paramedics. A lot of questions. But somehow Fergus and I finally get to be alone.

He takes my hand. We walk down to the dock, and we both sit cross-legged on the wood. For at least five minutes, we don't say anything at all.

Then Fergus slides his arm around my waist and tips his head so it rests on mine.

"Well," he says. "That was fun. But let's never do it again."

"That was the least fun thing *ever*," I say. "And yes. Let's never do it again."

"At least we'll have some fresh scars," he replies.

He shifts and holds out his arm. It's wrapped in white bandages covering new burns. I don't have anything quite as bad. But the guy from the ambulance did tell me the gash on my forehead will leave a mark.

"That's what life is, right?" Fergus adds. "Fresh scars on top of old ones?"

"How very wise of you," I tease.

"Why, thank you." He grins.

I smile back, but then I get serious again.

"Someone else might not have saved Andy," I say. "Not after what he did to you."

"But then I'd have to live with that," Fergus replies. "And I think I've got enough other guilt."

"Sal told me you and Andy set the fire the night your mom died," I say.

His mouth twists like he's tasted something sour. "Let me guess. She got that from Andy?"

I shrug because I still don't know how the story got shared.

"It's not true," he tells me. "It happened the way I said it did. But Andy likes to remember it differently. He needs someone to blame. He's always been like that. All of his problems were my fault. Not that I don't have a habit of doing shitty things. But Andy is his own worst enemy. He isn't at Camp Happy because of me."

"Can I ask you something?"

"You can ask me anything," he replies.

"If you didn't set the fire, how come *you're* here?"

"You gonna show me yours if I show you mine?" he asks.

I don't hesitate.

"It's not impressive," I warn. "If you were hoping for something badass, I'm afraid you're not going to get it."

"That's fine. Let me hear your non-badass story," he says.

"Lipstick."

"What?"

"I stole one from the grocery store," I reply. "Fifth count of petty theft. I was already on probation for the first four times. Then my mom OD'd. And when she got sent to rehab, it was either Camp Happy or juvie for me." I pause and nudge his shoulder. "Okay, your turn. Did you steal a lipstick too?"

"Slightly more badass than that," he admits. "And I'm not proud of it."

"Tell me anyway."

"Before my mom died, I was involved with some guys who boosted cars," he says. "After I got out of the hospital from my burn stuff, I knew I had to go straight. Some of the guys didn't like that. So I drove a car into one of their houses to prove a point. Bad choice."

"Was it a stolen car?"

"Maybe."

"Yeah, okay. I'd have sent you here too," I joke.

"Very funny," he replies. "And now I get to ask *you* something."

"Okay. Go for it."

"Why'd you come looking for me anyway? Even if you thought I might've set the fire that killed my mom, I mean."

I blush. "I like you. And besides, someone's past doesn't make them less worthy in the present."

Fergus lifts an eyebrow. "Oh, really?"

I frown at him. "What? What's with the look?"

"Repeat those words back to yourself," he replies. "Then apply it to your stuff with your dad."

I open my mouth. Then I close it. He's right. Or I guess *I'm* right. My past doesn't make me less worthy. And my dad will know that too.

Suddenly, despite everything, my whole body feels lighter.

"So what now?" says Fergus. "We still have almost a week of camp left."

"Do you actually think they're going to let us stay?"

"No." He laughs and shakes his head. "Well, maybe. They might have a hard time finding a place for us."

"Fergus…"

"Adele…"

"Even if we have to leave, like, today…we'll stay in touch, won't we?"

As a reply, he tips his mouth to mine and gives me one of his toe-curling kisses. And that's way better than words anyway.

Chapter Three

Most people have already gone in. I heard the first bell when I was seeing Jude off, but I know I still have a couple of minutes before the second bell. It doesn't really matter anyway, though, because it's my final year and most of my teachers know me well. I have a certain degree of freedom. They know about Jude and the complications of being her caregiver and trust me to get my work done. So I take this time to wander down the halls without hurrying. I run my fingers along the lockers, feeling the cold metal and listening to the sound of the locks shifting under my touch. I love that sound. The smell is wonderful too—pencil shavings and fresh paper, with an occasional whiff of body spray.

The halls are deserted, so it comes as a complete shock when I round the corner and almost run into someone. We both stop short. He smiles. I have never seen this boy before. He has the whitest, straightest teeth I have ever seen. His dark brown skin and closely shaved hair highlight the spiky red mohawk that runs all the way down to the back of his neck. He's wearing dress pants with suspenders and a Beatles T-shirt, *Yellow Submarine*, which just happens to be my favorite album. And his gray eyes are lined with just the slightest hint of black liner.

I have no words.

I smile back at him and then immediately flush with embarrassment.

"Hi," he says. His voice is low but delicate, like he's not quite used to the sound of it.

"Hi," I reply. I'm surprised I can even say that much. I'm not much for dating, because Jude takes up so much of my time. But it's not like I'm a robot. This guy is *hot*.

"I'm looking for B101," he says.

"You're new," I say, then shut my mouth quickly. What a stupid thing to say. Of course he's new. I *definitely* would have noticed him last year.

"Is it that obvious?" he says. He spreads his arms, palms up, and looks down at himself.

I laugh, but it comes out more like a bark. I smile to try to cover it up. He tilts his head at me and looks puzzled.

"Actually, I'm going to B101 right now," I say.

The second bell rings. It's so loud we both cover our ears. I'm usually in the classroom by second bell, so I'm not used to the volume of it bouncing around the empty halls.

"Physics?" he asks after the bell has finished.

"My favorite," I reply. I try to sound like I'm joking, but it comes out completely serious. I mean, I wasn't joking—I do love physics. But I was trying to keep it light in case he hates it and thinks I'm a giant nerd.

"I'm more into chemistry," he replies, "but it's all physics in the end, isn't it?"

I wait for a second to make sure he's not joking. But his smile is sincere. Have I died and gone to heaven?

"Yeah," I say. "I mean, I guess."

There's a moment of silence where we just stare at each other.

"So?" he asks, raising his eyebrows.

"What?"

"The classroom?"

"The class..." My brain is definitely not working.

"Like, where we sit in desks, write notes and listen to the teacher drone on about velocity?"

My eyes keep venturing down to his lips. It's hard to focus on the words he's saying. It takes me a second to snap out of it.

"The classroom. Yes." I start walking abruptly and almost bump into him. I'm not usually like this, I swear. But I can't seem to control the feeling that's pulsing though me. The boy with the funky hair and perfect smile turns to follow me. I notice that he has an earthy boy smell. I like it.

"I'm Jack, by the way," he says as we head toward the classroom.

"Jack," I say. "Cool. I'm Penny."

"Like Penny Lane?" he asks, laughing a little.

I look over my shoulder at him. He's walking slightly behind me but still keeping up. He locks eyes with me, and it makes me shiver. His gray eyes stand out against his dark brown skin. I've never seen eyes like his before.

"Yeah, actually," I reply.

His eyes open a little wider, and I feel like I could just fall right into them.

"Really? That's cool. I'm a fan, if you couldn't tell." He points to his T-shirt.

"I love *Yellow Submarine*," I say.

"Yeah, me too."

I look forward again just in time to see the door of B101. It would be just like me to miss it completely and make an even bigger ass of myself. I stop suddenly, and he bumps into me. We both laugh, and I point at the door.

"Classroom," I say.

He grins at me. "Classroom, good," he says like a caveman.

I laugh a little too loudly as he opens the door and waves me inside.

Melinda Di Lorenzo has been writing professionally for more than a decade. In 2013 she won Harlequin's annual *So You Think You Can Write* contest, which came with a publishing contract and launched her successfully into the romance world. Bullied as a teen, Melinda sought refuge in books. She now wants to bring that refuge to others, and she draws on her experience as the parent of three teens to craft stories that reflect modern struggles of flawed characters without turning those struggles into stereotypes. She also supports young writers and makes an annual creative writing scholarship donation to École Salish Secondary. She lives in Vancouver, British Columbia.